2/04

Bicycle Mystery

GERTRUDE CHANDLER WARNER

Illustrated by David Cunningham

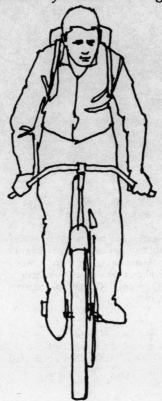

ALBERT WHITMAN & COMPANY

Chicago

ISBN 0-8075-0709-1

24

Printed in the U.S.A.

Contents

CHAPTER 1

Good Guess by Benny

The Alden family was up early on the first day of August. This was the day Mr. Alden was going to tell his four grandchildren about a plan he had made.

When Grandfather came into the dining room for breakfast, Henry, Jessie, Violet, and Benny were waiting.

Henry said, "I'm afraid there is not much time left. Making the tree house for our neighbors took more time than we thought."

"That's all right," Mr. Alden answered, sitting down. "My idea is for a very short trip. It won't take much time."

Benny sat down. "Then it *is* a trip," he said, smiling to himself. "A trip always means an adventure."

Jessie and Violet looked at each other.

"You might as well tell us now, Grandfather," said Jessie. She poured her grandfather's coffee.

"Thank you, my dear," said Mr. Alden. He put a lump of sugar into his cup. Benny began to think he could not wait another second. Then Grandfather looked up and smiled.

"Your Aunt Jane wrote to me early this summer," he said. "She would like to have you all come to see her on the farm. You can stay overnight. Anytime, she said, just let her know when you are coming so she can have plenty for Benny to eat."

Benny laughed. "Good for Aunt Jane," he said.

Henry said thoughtfully, "We like the farm, but there aren't many adventures left there for Benny to work on."

"No," agreed Mr. Alden. "That's why I thought you might like to find a new way to get to Aunt Jane's."

"You mean we won't take the station wagon?" Violet asked.

"We can't fly there," Henry said. "It is too short a trip to go by plane."

Jessie shook her head and said, "Well, how else can we go? I don't want to walk."

Benny began to laugh. "I know what you are thinking about, Grandfather," he said. "We could ride our bikes. It isn't too far for that."

"You guessed it," Mr. Alden agreed. "And who knows? You might ride your bikes right into an adventure."

"A bicycle adventure!" exclaimed Benny. "That's different. We wouldn't just whizz up to the farm in a car. We can take all the old back roads instead of the big highways. We can even take it easy and stay over-night along the way."

Mr. Alden nodded. "Yes," he said. "I have thought about that. There are motels where you can stay."

"That's wonderful, Grandfather," Jessie said. "No busy highways with cars racing by."

"Highways are OK if you're in a hurry," said Benny. "But we won't be in a hurry. We'll take our time. This will be fun. We can ride about fifty miles a day on our bikes if we have to."

Violet said, "Will you be all right alone, Grand-father?"

"Of course," answered Mr. Alden. "I won't be alone, anyway. I have plenty of people to look out for me. Don't worry. And remember I will keep Watch. He is too old a dog to run after four bikes."

"Let's see," began Jessie. "We can't take very much. We need one change of clothes, sweaters, and pajamas."

"Yes," agreed Violet. "We can wash things out and let them dry overnight."

Henry said, "A raincoat would be handy if it rains."

"And emergency rations," put in Benny. "It would be awful to have nothing to eat in an emergency."

Jessie agreed.

"How about sleeping bags?" Benny asked. "Maybe we might have to camp out some night. Or we could sleep in Aunt Jane's barn—that would be an adventure."

Jessie looked at Benny and smiled. "All right," she said. "I don't think we'll use them, but we can strap them on the back of our bikes. The other things will fit in our knapsacks."

"I'll take a road map," Henry said.

"Bring your knife with the can opener, Henry," Jessie suggested. "I think our lunches will be picnics."

Grandfather smiled to himself as he listened to his grandchildren making their plans. He asked, "When do you want to start?"

Benny laughed. "We've been so busy talking about what to take we haven't planned when to go."

It was Violet who said, "What about tomorrow morning right after breakfast? We can telephone Aunt Jane and Uncle Andy tonight. Will our trip take about a week, Henry?"

"Not any more than that," Henry said. "Going and coming."

Packing did not take much time. After all, there was not much the Aldens were taking with them.

Aunt Jane and Uncle Andy were delighted to hear about the plans for the bike trip. Aunt Jane said she would ask Maggie to cook all the things that Benny liked best.

The next morning the Aldens put their knapsacks on their backs. Everything else went on the carriers. They wheeled their bicycles around to the front door.

Grandfather and Mrs. McGregor, the housekeeper, stood on the front porch. Watch sat at their feet. He seemed to know he was going to stay at home. He did not mind. It was not his idea of fun to run after bicycles.

"Good-bye!" they called. "Don't worry about us."

The four Aldens wheeled down the driveway and looked back to wave again. Then they headed toward the river road.

When they were out of sight, Mrs. McGregor turned to go in. She said, "You have four grandchildren to be proud of, Mr. Alden. They know how to get themselves out of trouble without any help."

"Yes," agreed Mr. Alden. "They have always solved their own problems, just as they do mysteries. I hope Benny will find an adventure on this trip. But maybe he will run into trouble, too."

And Mr. Alden was right.

CHAPTER 2

First Aid

The sun was shining, and it was a beautiful morning. It was not too warm and not too cold.

"Remember how we came along this way in the station wagon when we were going on the houseboat?" Henry asked.

"That's right," Benny said. "What was the name of the first place where we stopped?"

"Wasn't it called Second Landing?" Violet asked. "I remember there was a store there."

"Let's stop again!" Benny said. "Maybe the man in the store will remember us."

"We can buy some things for lunch," Jessie said.

The Aldens liked the smooth country road. There were trees and bushes on both sides.

When they had ridden about ten miles, Benny said, "I think I see a railroad crossing. Maybe we are coming to a town."

When they were closer, Benny called out, "Yes, it's Second Landing. I remember it."

"And there is Mr. Martin's store," said Henry. "We bought groceries there for the houseboat."

The Aldens leaned their bicycles against the side of the little store. They went inside.

Right away they heard a woman's voice saying, "Oh, Mr. Martin, I'm so upset."

"I'm sorry, Mrs. Randall," said Mr. Martin. "I'd like to help you. Tell me about it." He nodded at the Aldens. "Be with you in a minute."

The children saw that Mrs. Randall was a pretty woman with curly brown hair. She was small, and she certainly was upset.

She said, "My husband is bringing his boss, Mr. Evans, home to supper. And I just got Carl off to camp, and the house is a mess. Now I have to get a special dinner and clean up the house and yard. And I have to do it alone."

Jessie went over to the counter. "Excuse me," she said. "We couldn't help hearing."

The woman turned around and saw the four young people.

Jessie said, "We'd like to help you out. We are just taking a bicycle trip. Violet and I would love to do your housework, and Henry and Benny could do your yard."

"That's right," Henry added. " We have plenty of time. We'll be glad to help you."

Mrs. Randall stood with her mouth open in surprise. Then she exclaimed, "How kind you are! I'm a perfect stranger. I could never let you do this."

"Oh, yes you could," said Benny. "Just try."

"Now you have some good help," said Mr. Martin. "I've met these Aldens and you can trust them."

"We are looking for an adventure, anyway," said Benny.

Mr. Martin laughed. "It looks like a lot of hard work to me."

"If you really mean it—" began Mrs. Randall.

"Of course we mean it," said Benny. "And here we stand, wasting time."

"All right!" said Mrs. Randall. "I'll do it! I'm buying things for a boiled dinner."

Violet said, "That's good. That is the dinner my grandfather likes best."

Mr. Martin was already putting things in bags.

"Give them to me," Henry said. "We'll carry the bags on our bikes."

"Oh, you don't need bikes," said Mrs. Randall. "I live just around the corner."

Benny said, "We have to take our bikes anyway. We might as well take the groceries, too."

They rode along slowly, and Mrs. Randall walked. "Right here," she said, pointing. The boys saw that the grass needed cutting. She opened the door.

Mrs. Randall led the way into the kitchen, saying, "It was awfully good of you to come. Have you had lunch?"

"No," answered Benny, "and I am starving!"

Mrs. Randall laughed and said, "You make me think of my son Carl. He's always hungry."

She stopped smiling suddenly and looked worried.

"That's funny," the Aldens thought. "Her troubles should be over."

"Why is she worrying when there are four people to help her?" wondered Jessie.

Then Jessie took peanut butter and bread out of the bag and began to make sandwiches. Mrs. Randall said, "If I can't make sandwiches for you, I can give you milk and bananas."

Henry set four chairs at the kitchen table. As Mrs. Randall watched them eat, she said, "I can't believe you are going to help. It seems like a dream."

"I'm no dream," said Benny. "Just touch me." They all laughed, and everyone felt better.

When lunch was over, the girls began to wash the breakfast and lunch dishes. The boys went out into the yard.

"You'll find rakes and things in the garage," Mrs. Randall called after them. "Don't touch the—" She stopped. "But then you wouldn't anyway."

Henry and Benny looked at each other. "Now what do you make of that?" Benny asked. "I feel that something is still wrong, but I can't think what."

"Neither can I," said Henry. "Of course, we are strangers. Maybe we will find out later."

Then all was quiet for awhile except for the noise of the dishes and the lawnmower. Mrs. Randall went upstairs to make the beds. She had left all the things to make a boiled dinner. Corned beef, cabbage, carrots, and turnips lay on the table.

Jessie and Violet began to peel the vegetables. Then they put everything into a big kettle. Later they would add the potatoes.

Mrs. Randall came downstairs. She said, "This has to boil slowly for a long time."

"But then your whole dinner is done," said Jessie.

"Except for a pie," Violet said. "Mrs. Randall, let Jessie make an apple pie for you. I'll peel the apples."

"I'm sure any man would like that," said Mrs. Randall. "I should tell you that my husband sounded nervous this morning when he telephoned me from Boston. He doesn't have any idea why Mr. Evans wants to see him. He could see him any time in Boston. Perhaps he isn't doing his work very well."

Benny came in just in time to hear this. "Then again," he said, "maybe Mr. Evans is going to give your husband a better job and more money."

Mrs. Randall laughed. "That could be. But why does Mr. Evans want to visit us in our home?"

"There must be some reason," Jessie said. "I guess we'll have to wait and see."

Mrs. Randall went into the dining room to dust. Suddenly Violet noticed that she was sitting down at the table with her head on her hand.

"Are you all right?" she asked anxiously.

Mrs. Randall jumped up and said brightly, "Oh, yes, I was just resting."

But Violet thought, "She is still worrying about something."

Later, the girls helped Mrs. Randall get ready for company. Violet said, "This must be your boy's slipper." She held up an old green slipper, ripped along one side. "I found it behind the sofa."

"Yes, it's Carl's," Mrs. Randall said. "I'm afraid he isn't very neat."

"Like most boys," said Jessie, laughing.

Mrs. Randall laughed, too, but she soon looked sad again. Violet thought to herself, "Something is wrong. I'm sure it has something to do with Carl."

When the table was set, Mrs. Randall said, "The men will come on the six o'clock train. I'll go upstairs and change my dress."

But the Aldens could hear her saying to herself, "Oh, dear! Oh, dear me!" They looked at each other.

"Still worrying," Jessie said to Henry.

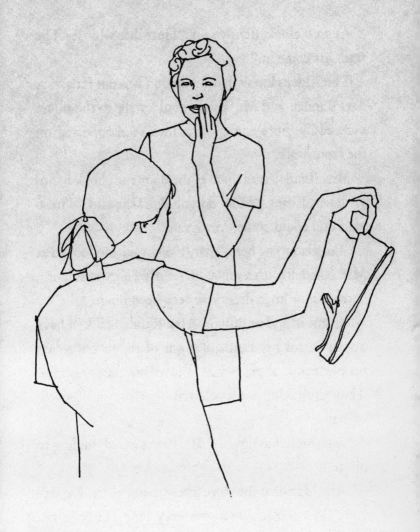

At six o'clock, Benny said, "Hear that whistle? The train has come in."

The Aldens knew that the station was not far away. Mr. Randall and Mr. Evans could walk to the house very easily. Sure enough, the men soon appeared on the front walk.

Mrs. Randall met them at the door and shook hands with Mr. Evans. "How do you do?" she said. "I'm so glad you could come, Mr. Evans."

"I'm glad to be here," Mr. Evans said and looked at Mrs. Randall with a smile. Her curly hair was smooth, and her blue linen dress was very becoming.

"Come in and sit down," Mrs. Randall said. "I have a surprise for my husband. Four of the nicest young people came along when I was buying groceries. They are taking a bicycle trip, but they offered to help me."

"You mean strangers?" Mr. Evans asked, smiling to himself.

"Mr. Martin at the store knew them," Mrs. Randall said. "We weren't strangers very long. They're my friends now." And she introduced the Aldens to Mr. Evans and her husband.

Mr. Evans said, "Can I believe my nose? I smell something I haven't had for years. A New England boiled dinner!"

"Good!" Mrs. Randall exclaimed. "I'm so glad you like that. And Jessie made us an apple pie. You don't know what wonderful friends the Aldens have been to me!"

"You are having dinner with us, aren't you?" Mr. Randall said to the Aldens.

Henry shook his head. "We'd like to, sir, but we think we should be on our way. There's a motel between here and Ashby. That's where we plan to stay tonight."

"I asked them to stay to dinner and overnight, too," Mrs. Randall said. "But they wouldn't. Maybe you'll stop on your way back?"

Jessie smiled. "That's right. Maybe we will. We have had such a good time with you."

Mr. Evans said, "I'm sorry you young people can't

stay. I'm sure you are all wondering why I came. I was going to tell the Randalls later, but if you are going, I'll tell it now. It has a lot to do with the Aldens."

Everyone looked puzzled. Mr. Evans had never heard of the Aldens until that very day.

However, Mr. Evans went on. "Mr. Randall is doing an excellent job for me. He is the right man, and he makes friends easily. I want to give him a more important place in the company. But first I had to be sure that his wife also makes friends easily. I see that she does! I hope you will both be happy about moving to Boston."

Mrs. Randall's eyes were dancing as she looked at Jessie. She said, "See what you did for me!"

Mr. Randall said, "This is great news! And you never need to worry about my wife. She is more friendly than I am."

The Aldens shook hands with Mr. and Mrs. Randall and Mr. Evans, and got ready to pedal away. They all waved good-bye.

The riders soon left Second Landing behind them. The wind blowing on their backs seemed to be pushing them along.

Henry looked at his watch. "We have about two hours before it will be dark," he said.

"Do you think we have to wait until we get to the motel to eat?" Benny asked.

"No, we'll stop at the first good place we see," Henry promised. "We're all hungry."

As the Aldens rode along, Jessie said, "Oh, I love these country roads. And we've already had an adventure for you, Ben."

"And a real mystery, too," said Benny. "A mystery about Mrs. Randall and her son Carl. Something was wrong."

Violet said, "And it had nothing to do with company for supper."

"Right," said Jessie.

The Aldens had been riding for half an hour when Henry said, "Look, there's a restaurant."

"A good thing, too," said Benny. "I'm starved."

An hour later the Aldens had finished dinner and were coming out of the restaurant to get their bikes.

"It looks like rain to me," said Violet. "Look at those black clouds. We'd better hurry."

Benny didn't know it, but he was hurrying toward another adventure on their bicycle trip.

CHAPTER 3

Out of the Rain

Indeed very suddenly it did look like rain. The clouds began to pile up and turn black. Before the Aldens could go anywhere to spend the night it began to rain. Then it began to pour. The rain came down in sheets. The thunder roared.

"Oh, dear," called Jessie. "Let's find some shelter. We can't get to the motel in this rain. We'll be soaking wet."

"I'm soaking wet now," Benny said. "Raincoats are no good."

Henry called, "Just watch for any old shed. The water is dripping off my nose and ears."

"We might find a haystack," said Benny. "That would be like the days in the boxcar."

Violet pushed back her wet hair. "A haystack would be soaking wet, too."

The Aldens watched both sides of the road as they pedaled along. Then they saw the old house.

It was set back from the road, among some trees. Not a soul was around. Every window in the house was broken, and the door was banging in the wind.

"There!" called Benny. "There's your old house. It's got a roof, anyway."

Henry said, "I'm sure the roof leaks, but that won't make much difference when every window is broken. I'll go first and you follow me."

"No," said Benny firmly. I'll go with you. We'll go together and scare out the ghosts."

They all laughed, for they knew there were no

ghosts. The two boys pushed the door back and looked into a big room. There was nothing in the room, not even a carpet.

"Nobody here," called Henry. "You girls get off your bikes and push them right in." He and Benny set their own bikes in a corner and looked around.

"Well, the roof doesn't leak," said Jessie. "And this side of the room away from the windows isn't wet at all."

"Just a little damp," said Benny. "But no puddles to sit in. Let's stay here on the dry side and look at our new mansion."

Violet looked at the bare room and said, "I'm sure the owner of this house won't mind if we stay here until it stops raining."

"I don't think the owner cares about his house," said Henry. "We can't hurt it anyway."

The rain still blew in the windows, and the water began to run into a corner.

Benny said, "I wish that water knew enough to run out the front door."

Henry replied, "Well, Ben, if the water rises too high, we can go upstairs. In fact, I think I'll go up and see what it looks like."

Henry had plenty of company. They all went upstairs to find two empty rooms and a bathroom.

"But the bathroom is no good," said Benny. "The pipes are all broken."

"Nobody here for a long time," Henry said.

Jessie looked at the tub. She said, "This might be a good place to dry our clothes, though. See that rod over the tub? Once they must have had a shower curtain."

"Good," said Henry. "Let's look at the rest of the house."

The rain came in only at the front, just as it did on the first floor.

"These were the bedrooms," said Violet. "I do wonder why the owner doesn't fix this up. It's a lovely old house."

Jessie answered, "I don't think the owner has been around here for a long time."

"It's getting dark and I'm hungry," said Benny. "How about having a little something to eat?"

"There! I was just waiting for you to say that, Ben," said his brother. "There's no electricity, and we certainly don't want to eat by a flashlight. Let's eat now while we can still see."

"Wait a minute," said Jessie. "We all have dry clothes in our packs, and we each have a towel. Let's get dry first. We can put on our dry clothes and hang the wet ones on the rod over the bathtub."

"That's all right with me," said Benny. "It won't take long. I'll be the first one ready."

And he was. The girls laughed as they heard him clattering down the wooden stairs.

"We'll have to go to bed early tonight," Jessie said, "if we want to see our way. And we'll eat our emergency rations. I never really thought we would use them. I thought we could always get to a motel. But here we are in the pouring rain, and no motel."

Benny was taking out the emergency rations when his sisters came downstairs.

Violet said suddenly, "Remember the boxcar days? Put down one paper napkin for a tablecloth and save every crumb. If we leave crumbs, we'll surely have mice."

"We could have anything," Benny said cheerfully. "Anything could get through the broken windows. Even a bear."

"No bears in this part of the country," said Violet peacefully. "But we could have mice if we leave crumbs."

Four napkins were soon laid on the floor, and the Aldens began to eat.

Jessie said, "We'd better save some food for breakfast. It may not stop raining. Save some of the milk and crackers."

"That's right," said Henry. "Benny always has to eat before he goes anywhere."

"Even to bed," said Benny. He yawned.

There was no trouble about the crumbs. They ate every one. The rain still poured down and blew in at the front windows.

Henry was thinking. He said, "You girls sleep upstairs. Ben and I will put our sleeping bags down here. We'd better sleep in our clothes."

"You were right, Benny," Jessie said. "We do need our sleeping bags after all."

"But I thought we'd be sleeping out," Benny said.

After their exciting day, the Aldens went to sleep without any trouble. The rain still pounded on the roof, but they were safe and dry.

But just as it was getting light in the morning, Jessie and Violet were wakened by a noise downstairs. It sounded like an animal whining.

"What's the matter, Henry?" Jessie called down the stairs.

"Well, you might say we have a visitor. A dog wants to come in the window."

Jessie and Violet then heard Benny laugh softly. "At least we think it's a dog. He barks anyway. He has come in the window already."

The dog went on whining, but it was a different sort of whining. Once in a while the dog gave a bark.

Violet turned to Jessie. "Let's go downstairs and see what kind of dog we have. He doesn't seem to be very happy."

"I don't blame him," said Jessie. "It's still raining. No dog would be very happy in this pouring rain. But I should think he'd be glad to get in the house."

The girls went downstairs.

They looked at the dog. They saw that it was small and smoky gray. Hair hung down all over his face and bright black eyes. His tail was wagging, and he was trying to climb up Benny's legs.

"Come here, dog," said Jessie. The dog turned around instantly and trotted over to Jessie.

"Oh," said Benny, "an obedient dog."

"Yes," said Jessie with a nod. "I think he has had some training. Sit!" The dog sat down.

"Well, well," said Henry. "Come! Heel!"

The dog trotted over to Henry's left side and looked up at him. Henry began to walk around the room. The dog followed him just behind his left foot.

"He minds better than some children," said Violet.

Henry turned around and the dog turned around. "Sit!" said Henry, and the dog sat down.

Then Henry said, "Stay!" and walked back to the others. The dog did not move. But he didn't stop whining.

"Maybe he's hurt," Henry said. "Come here, fellow." The dog came over to him once more. Henry looked him all over and felt the dog's ears and legs. At last he said, "He seems to be all right."

Jessie took the little dog in her lap and felt his neck. "My, he's soft," she said. She hugged him, and he licked her hand. She said, "No, I don't think he's hurt."

Suddenly Jessie noticed something. "That's strange," she said. "He doesn't have any collar."

"He's just a stray dog," said Benny. "He'll probably go along soon."

"I don't think he's a stray dog," said Henry. "I think he belongs to somebody. Somebody must have trained him to obey. And somebody loved him."

The little dog put his head on one side and looked

up at Henry out of one bright eye.

"Oh, look at him!" Violet said. "He's so cute when he does that. Do you suppose we can find his owner?"

Henry looked thoughtful. "I'd say he has to do that for himself. Let's see what he does when we get ready to start off on our bikes."

Benny said, "No collar, no tag, no anything. We don't even know his name. Not much to go on."

"You're right, Ben," said Jessie. "Nothing to go on."

Violet said, "Somehow I don't want to go back to bed."

Henry laughed. "We all know the answer to that. As Ben would say, 'Let's have breakfast!' "

CHAPTER 4

Sunshine and Shadow

Listen!" said Violet. "It isn't raining as hard this morning as it was last night. Maybe it will stop soon."

"It's only six o'clock," said Henry. "But we should be on our way as soon at it stops raining."

"This won't be much of a breakfast," said Jessie as they sat down on the floor.

"What about our new dog?" Benny asked. "He's got to eat, too."

"Let's each give him a part of our breakfast," said Jessie. "He'll have enough."

It was a good idea, but it was hard to give up some of their small breakfast. They felt better, though, when they saw how hungry the dog was.

"Don't eat so fast, dog," Benny exclaimed. "Make it last."

But the dog had no idea of making it last. He snapped up his share of crackers and milk. Then he looked up for more.

"I don't think he's had anything to eat for at least a day," said Violet.

Henry put his things away and stood up. "Look, it's stopped raining," he said. "We must find a place where we can get a real breakfast. And then we must see who has lost a dog."

"Yes," agreed Jessie. "I think something is wrong with him. Listen! He still whines. He must belong to somebody."

The Aldens packed up all their things. They strapped the sleeping bags on the back of their bikes.

"We can't say good-bye to anybody," said Benny. "And we can't lock the door."

The four Aldens took their bikes and went out of the old house. Henry shut the front door as well as he could. Then they walked their bikes along the wet path to the road.

"That dog is going to follow us," said Benny.

"We shouldn't let him," said Jessie firmly. "We've got one dog at home, and Watch wouldn't like another. And besides, I still think he must live nearby. See? His paws don't look sore, and they would if he had come a long way."

Jessie looked down at the little dog and he just wagged his tail. "Go home!" she said. "That's a good dog, go home now. Go home!"

But the dog did not go home. He stood still in the path and watched the Aldens. When they got on their bikes, the dog followed them.

Benny said, "Don't pay any attention to him.

Maybe he'll trot off home. And the first one who sees a store gets a dime."

Henry went first and Violet last. The little dog ran along behind Violet's bike.

"We must find a place to eat, and a store to buy more emergency rations," Jessie said.

"Maybe we'll find them both at the same place," Violet said. "I hope so."

The Aldens passed several houses, but they saw no people. The dog followed them, still whining.

At last the children saw a building that looked like a country store.

"We all saw the store at the same time," said Jessie. "Nobody gets the dime."

It was a store, but it wasn't open. The Aldens sat down on the steps and waited. The dog sat beside them and waited, too.

"After all, it's not seven yet," said Jessie. "Maybe the store doesn't open until eight."

"Well, if it's eight," said Benny, "I shall die of starvation."

But the store did not open at eight. It was seven o'clock when a man came down the road, taking a key out of his pocket.

"Hi, kids!" he said. "What can I do for you?"

The dog whined and the Aldens all jumped up.

"We want a lot of things," said Benny. "But first we want to buy something to eat right away."

The man put the key in the door and opened it.

"Look around," said the storekeeper. "But that doesn't mean your dog! See that he doesn't get into anything."

Benny said, "Come. Sit." The dog trotted to Benny and sat down.

"Well, some dog!" the man exclaimed. "I wish my children minded me like that."

"You don't know this dog, then?" Henry asked. "He isn't ours. He just followed us."

"Never saw him before in my life," the man answered.

"He can't live very far away," said Henry. "See? His feet aren't sore. He hasn't come a long way."

"Maybe somebody dropped him out of a car. It's a mean thing to do, but some people do it," said the storekeeper. "You can be sure that dog never came from around here. He's a funny looking dog. I never saw one just like him. I'll ask around, but I'm sure nobody will know about him."

"We don't want to keep him," Benny said. "We've already got a good dog at home."

"Watch wouldn't be very pleased to see a strange dog," Henry said. "Especially a dog that minds when Watch never minds any more." Everyone laughed.

Jessie was busy picking out more supplies for their emergency rations. Then she started on things for breakfast.

The man kindly washed out the four Thermos bottles and filled them with milk. Jessie bought bread, two extra bottles of milk, butter, cereal, and bananas.

"Here's a good bone for your dog," the man said.

"Oh, thank you!" said Jessie. "I suppose we'll have to take him with us. But every minute I feel we are taking him farther away from his home."

"Too bad," said the man, shaking his head. "I can't keep him here. I don't want a dog around my store. You'll have to take him with you."

There was nothing else to do. The pretty little whining dog ran along with the Aldens on their bicycles.

Benny said, "We don't know what his real name is. But I have a name for him. We ought to call him

Shadow. He follows us just like a shadow."

Violet added, "And he's blue-gray, like a shadow."

From that moment, the dog's name was Shadow.

"There are a lot of good places along here for a picnic breakfast," Jessie called back.

"I hope no cows," called Violet.

Benny looked at the field they were passing. "No, nothing but daisies, Violet. Not a cow."

The Aldens rode along, finding only one hill where they had to get off and walk. Then they saw just the right field. There were bushes and trees to hide them from the road, and there was a big flat rock for a table.

Soon the bikes were lying on the grass, and the family was sitting around the stone table.

"I wish I had some butter for my bread," Benny said.

"I did buy some, Ben," said Jessie. "I bought just enough for breakfast. It won't keep in the hot sun."

The sun was out, and everyone was happy. Shadow sat down without being told and waited politely.

Jessie poured some milk for him in a paper plate.
Then she broke up some bread and dropped it in the
milk.

"You can have your bone for lunch," she said.

The Aldens started to eat their cereal and bananas
and milk. "No banana for Shadow," Benny said,
laughing. "But what are we going to do with him,
Henry?"

"I really don't know," replied Henry. "He must
live somewhere around here. With us, he's getting
farther away all the time. But it can't be helped."

So Shadow followed his new family when they
started on.

CHAPTER 5

Eight Helping Hands

Now that breakfast was over, Benny said, "My, I feel good. I feel like having an adventure. I only wish our shadow would stop whining. Shadow, don't you know that shadows don't whine?"

But Shadow paid no attention. He ran along, whining softly.

Violet said to Benny, "I don't know why you want another adventure. I'd say we have had an adventure already—not to say a mystery."

"Well, I like adventures all the time," replied Benny. "Now look—isn't that a vegetable stand up the road? It has a big red sign. Now that's interesting."

"There's a boy selling vegetables," Jessie said, looking down the road.

Then the Aldens saw a man carrying a basket from a field to the roadside stand. He walked slowly, and seemed tired.

"Why doesn't that boy help?" Benny asked.

They all found the answer when they rode up to the stand. The boy had one leg in a cast. A pair of crutches stood in the corner of the shed behind him.

The boy saw the Aldens looking at him. "I fell in the barn and broke my leg," he told them.

"Oh," said Violet. "I'm sorry."

"I'll be all right," the boy said. "But the trouble is that my father needs my help right now. All I can do is keep the stand open for him. I can't help with the picking and carrying."

The boy stopped talking and looked worried.

"Could you use a little help?" asked Henry. "We are just passing through."

"Did you say help?" exclaimed the boy. He could not believe his ears. "What do you mean, help?"

"We mean just what we say," said Henry, and the other Aldens all nodded. He got off his bike and the rest did the same. "We'll be glad to help you if you tell us what to do."

The man and the boy stared. Then the man said slowly, "I never heard anything like this. We've got work enough if you really mean it."

For answer, the Aldens wheeled their bikes behind the stand.

The father said, "I have ripe tomatoes, cabbages, and beans to pick. It's more than I can do alone."

Jessie said, "Violet and I can pick beans. We know how to do that."

Henry said, "Show me how to cut the cabbages and I'll work at that."

"That leaves me with the tomatoes," Benny said. "I like tomatoes the best, anyway."

"How much do you charge?" the man asked.

"Nothing," replied Henry. "We are just passing through on a bicycle trip. My brother Benny was looking for an adventure. We'll call this an adventure."

"I'd call it hard work," the man said. That made the Aldens smile. It was exactly what Mr. Martin at Second Landing had said when they offered to help Mrs. Randall.

The man went on, "My name is Smith. I guess you can remember that. You mean to tell me that anybody does something for nothing nowadays?"

Benny said, "We like to, Mr. Smith. Especially during vacation. My name's Benny Alden. These are my sisters and my brother Henry."

The boy was about Benny's age. He said, "My name is Roy. I wish I could go along with you."

Violet looked at Roy and had an idea. "I know what you can do to help," she said. "I don't think our dog Shadow should follow us into the garden. Why don't you keep him here with you?"

Roy patted the dog and Shadow wagged his tail. He was a friendly little dog.

"I never saw a dog like this before," the boy said. "What kind is it?"

"We don't know," Benny answered. Then he told how Shadow had come to them during the rainstorm.

"He just sticks right with us," Benny finished. "That's why we call him Shadow."

"But we wish we could find his owner," Jessie said.

"Well, Shadow and I will keep the stand," Roy said.

"Stay!" Henry told the dog, and Shadow sat down. Mr. Smith led the way to the garden.

Soon there were five workers instead of one. Mr. Smith began to look happier. With the Aldens' help, the work went quickly.

Some customers drove up just as the Aldens came from the garden with a load of fresh vegetables for Roy's stand. The customers could see how fresh the beans and the cabbages and the tomatoes were. They bought several bags full.

The sun was warm and pleasant after the rain. Everything smelled sweet with the hay in the next field.

Once when they were working in the garden Mr. Smith stopped to listen. He asked Benny, "Does that dog whine all the time?"

"Yes, he does," answered Benny. "Even when he should be happy, he whines. That's why we think he has a good home. But maybe someone went away and left him."

"I don't think so," Mr. Smith said. "I can remember seeing a picture of a dog like that in a magazine. I can't remember what kind he was, but I know a dog like that is worth a lot of money. If the owner didn't want him, he could sell him."

"Too bad he can't talk," Benny said. "He could tell us what happened and we could take him home."

"Anyway," Mr. Smith said, "we can feed him. It is time for lunch. Come on, we'll have lunch. You're hungry, aren't you?"

"I'm always hungry," Benny said.

But Jessie said, "I'm not sure we ought to stay. You can't feed four extra people like this."

Roy heard what Jessie said and answered, "Oh, yes, we can. My dad is a good cook. He's got a stew on the stove this minute. We can eat any time."

Jessie gave in. She saw that Mr. Smith really wanted

to pay them in some way for their help. And she was just as hungry as Benny.

Mr. Smith and the Aldens washed their hands in cold water at the pump. Then they went into the farm kitchen. Roy and Shadow stayed outdoors at the stand.

Mr. Smith set five plates of stew on the table. He said, "The stew is too hot for the dog. I'll set his out to cool. After we eat, you can take it to him. Then Roy can come in and eat."

The Aldens and Mr. Smith sat down to lunch. Henry told him how Shadow had found them in the old house.

"That house is on the back road," said Mr. Smith. "It doesn't help much in finding the dog's home."

After lunch they all went back to the stand with Shadow's plate.

Roy said, "Let me tell you a funny thing that happened while you were gone."

"What was it?" Benny asked quickly.

"Well, a pickup truck came along and stopped.

The man got out and bought some vegetables. But in the back of the truck, sitting on the floor, were twin girls about six years old. They looked just alike, and they were dressed alike, only one was dressed in pink and one was dressed in blue. All at once they saw Shadow sitting there. The girl in pink said, 'Oh, look! There's the very dog we saw in the parking lot!' "

"Parking lot!" repeated Benny. "I wonder what parking lot?"

"I don't know," said Roy. "It took me by surprise. The twin in blue called to him, 'Come, doggie, doggie,' and the one in pink snapped her fingers."

"I bet Shadow never moved," exclaimed Benny.

"Right," said Roy. "He just sat still. Henry had told him to stay, and he stayed. He did wag his tail, though. I noticed that."

Jessie asked, "Do you think he knew the little girls?"

"Yes, I think he did," answered Roy. "But not very well. They didn't know his name. They probably just saw him running around in some parking lot."

"Oh, dear," said Violet. "If we only knew where the parking lot was, we could find Shadow's owner."

Jessie was thoughtful. "It does help a little. It shows that the twins live rather near here."

"No, I don't think so." Roy shook his head. "We have had this vegetable stand for three years. And I never saw the pickup truck before or the man or the twin girls."

Henry said, "Mr. Smith, how would you begin if you had to find Shadow's owner?"

Both Mr. Smith and Roy laughed. Mr. Smith replied, "I'd try Miss Lucy at the post office. She knows everything. If anyone around here has lost a dog, she will know all about it."

"We'll ask her," Benny said. "Where is the post office?"

"About two houses down this road," said Roy, still laughing. "Have a good time!"

Henry said, "We have to be on our way now. My map shows that we have to ride about ten miles to find a motel where we can spend the night."

"That's right," agreed Mr. Smith. "That will be in the town of Ashby. It's a good motel, and it has a dining room. Thank you for your help."

"And thank you for the delicious lunch," said Jessie. "I see that Shadow has licked his plate clean."

When the Aldens reached Miss Lucy at the post office, they saw why Roy had laughed. Miss Lucy was a thin, sharp-eyed lady.

"No," she said. "I know every dog and cat and rabbit and horse and cow in this town, and I know nobody has lost a dog. I never saw such a comical looking animal."

"Well, thank you just the same," said Jessie. "If you ever hear of a lost dog, tell Mr. Smith at the vegetable stand. We left our names with his son Roy."

"I will," said Miss Lucy. "But you can be sure nobody around here would own a dog like that. That dog ought to go to a dog show, or more likely, a circus!"

"When they were out of sight of the post office, Benny said, "You know I don't think Shadow is that funny looking. I think he's beautiful. People just aren't used to him, that's all."

And so the Aldens pedaled along the quiet country road. But Shadow still whined.

CHAPTER 6

Trouble on the Road

When the Aldens had wheeled away from the post office, Henry said, "Now you can run awhile, Shadow. It will do you good. You are getting lazy."

The day was warm, and a little wind was blowing. It was a perfect day for riding. Shadow ran along beside Benny's bike and seemed to enjoy himself.

Benny was a little ahead of the others. Suddenly he stopped his bike and got off. He walked over to a sign nailed to a fence post.

"What do you know?" Benny said. "This might be fun."

Violet saw Benny stop and called, "What is it, Benny?"

"Look at this," Benny said as the others rode up. "It says there's going to be a dog show in Ashby on August 10."

Jessie said, "It seems to me that I saw a sign like that back in Second Landing."

"You did?" asked Benny. "Why didn't you tell me?"

Jessie laughed. "Well, I didn't know you were interested in dog shows, Benny. Anyway, that was before we had a dog."

"That's right," Benny agreed. "I guess I wouldn't have noticed this sign if Shadow weren't around. Anyway, it would be fun to see a dog show. Maybe we'd find out what kind of a dog Shadow is."

"We can do that anyway," Henry said. "I'm sure anybody from a kennel could tell us."

"It could be easier than that," Violet said. "There's probably a book in the library that has pictures of dogs like Shadow. It would tell us what kind he is."

Jessie said, "If they are having a big dog show in Ashby, there must be a lot of people around here who are interested in dogs."

Benny was thinking. He looked from the poster to Shadow. At last he said, "Oh, Shadow, I wish you could talk. Then we'd know whether you ran away from home or somebody stole you."

"Come on!" Jessie called. "We aren't going to get to Ashby and certainly not to Aunt Jane's if we stop here too long."

"All right!" Benny answered. "I'll race you, Jessie, to that big tree."

"Watch out for cars!" called Violet after them.

"There's nothing coming," Benny called back. And he and Shadow and Jessie were off.

Benny rode fast, but Jessie passed him.

Jessie won the race. "But I'm older than you, Ben," she said. She jumped off her bicycle at the tree and stood there, waiting for the others to come up.

Shadow was tired out when he caught up with Jessie. Nobody had to tell Shadow to sit. He was glad to rest.

When Henry and Violet rode up, they jumped off their bikes and sat down on the grass by the side of the road.

Very soon they saw a car coming in the distance. A woman was sitting beside the driver. As it came nearer, Benny said, "I think it is slowing down."

Jessie said, "That's funny. I think they are going to speak to us."

Jessie was right. The car stopped and the man got out. He was looking at the dog. The Aldens stood up beside their bikes to see what the man wanted.

The man said to Henry, "You have a fine dog there."

"Yes, we think so," answered Henry.

"Did you know he was a very rare dog?"

"No."

"I'd like to buy him," the man said.

Benny said, "We can't sell him. He isn't ours. He just follows us, and we are trying to find his owner."

"Well, if he doesn't belong to anybody, let me have him," the man said. "I'll pay you well for him. He's a young show dog."

Benny shook his head. "No, we couldn't sell anything we don't own. Besides, we are going to find out who does own him."

"Then this really isn't your dog?" the man said again. The Aldens didn't like the sound of his voice at all.

"No," Henry answered. "We are just trying to find his owner."

The man asked, "How do you plan to do that?"

Benny said, "Everywhere we go, we ask if anyone has lost a dog."

Henry added, "And when we get home, we'll put a lost-and-found notice in the newspaper."

The woman called to her husband, "Come on, the children aren't going to sell the dog."

Shadow gave a short bark at the strange man and then began to whine. Benny stooped down and picked up the little dog. Jessie reached over and petted Shadow while Benny held him.

The man said to the Aldens, "Well, don't let anything happen to that dog." And after a moment the strange couple drove off toward Ashby.

The Aldens picked up their bicycles and watched the car until it was out of sight.

"Well, well! What do you make of that?" asked Jessie.

"Not much," said Henry.

"I don't like it at all," said Violet. "Those people tried to make us feel as if we had done something wrong."

"Well, we know we haven't," Benny said cheerfully. "I think *they* are the ones who want to do something wrong. Let's forget them!"

"That's the best idea I have heard for a long while," said Jessie. "Let's go! We'll have to ride right along if we want to get to that good motel."

The Aldens rode along quietly for about a mile. Then Violet said, "I thought that woman took a picture of Shadow."

"So did I," said Jessie.

Benny said, "I heard a little click when the man got into the car."

"Well, never mind," said Henry. "A snapshot of Shadow won't hurt us."

And not one of the Aldens thought that the woman might have taken a picture of them, too, with their four bicycles.

CHAPTER 7

Danger in the Night

At about five o'clock the Aldens reached the Ashby motel where they planned to stay. They rode up to the office window with their strange dog. They asked for two rooms side by side, with a door between. The manager looked out and saw the dog.

"You can't keep a dog in your room, you know," the manager said. "It's against the rules."

"Oh, dear!" said Jessie. "Then we can't stay here. We have to keep the dog with us."

Henry turned to Shadow and said, "Sit." The dog sat down.

"Oho!" said the manager. "An obedient dog. Does he mind you when you tell him to stop whining?"

Henry laughed. "You know, we never tried that."

Just then Shadow made a whining sound. Benny went over and got down on one knee. The dog looked up at Benny through all the gray hair covering its face. He stopped whining, and then he began again.

Benny said, "Shadow, you can't stay if you whine."

Shadow whined.

"NO!" said Benny sharply. "No!" He shook his head at the dog. Shadow started to whine, but Benny took hold of his nose and held it tight. The little dog did not like this at all. He tried to whine once more.

Benny shouted at the top of his voice, "NO!"

Shadow had never heard anyone yell at him like that. He seemed to understand what Benny was trying to teach him. He put his head on one side and looked up at the manager. It seemed as if the dog wanted to show how well he could obey.

"He does look cute when he does that," the manager said. "I'll tell you what I'll do. You understand dogs are not allowed in the motel. But that dog minds so well I will give you two rooms on the very end, 199 and 200. You keep him in the little hallway. But if he whines, out he goes."

"And out we go, too," said Benny. "You hear that, Shadow? And that would be too bad, because I'm hungry."

Violet said, "You have a lovely dining room." The Aldens could see people eating dinner.

"Yes, it's a new dining room," the manager said. "We are serving dinner now. You can eat right away if you want."

"We do want," said Benny. "Yes, sir! We'll just go and leave our things in the rooms."

"And leave the dog," added the man. "I have an idea for him." He laughed to himself. The Aldens knew that whatever the idea was, it was a good one.

The man gave Henry two keys and showed him the way to go. "Park your bikes at the very end, around the corner," he said.

Shadow trotted along after his new family. The manager watched, still smiling.

When Henry unlocked the door of the room he and Benny would have, he found a little square hallway. He threw his raincoat on the floor and said to Shadow, "Lie down. Stay!"

Shadow lay down on the raincoat and looked up at Henry without a sound.

"Good dog," said Benny. "And don't you whine, remember! We'll bring you some supper after we have had ours."

"You talk to that dog as if he could understand every word," Violet said.

"Maybe he does," replied Benny. "You can't tell."

The Aldens did not stop to unpack. They just washed their hands and went out again.

"Stay!" Henry said to the dog. Then he went out and locked the door.

The Aldens walked over to the motel dining room and went in. Everything was bright and new. The manager was busy at the end of the dining room, but he smiled when he saw the Aldens. They found a table and sat down.

"This is the best place we have seen yet," said Jessie. "I'm going to have a real dinner."

They took their time.

At last Benny said, "That was delicious. I could ride twenty miles now."

"Tomorrow," said Jessie.

The manager came over and whispered to Henry. He gave him a brown paper bag. "Here's your dog's dinner," he said. "There's enough for his breakfast, too. Just don't let anyone see that you are feeding a dog."

"You are very kind," Jessie said. "We won't forget this."

"Well, I would not do this for everybody, but you seem like good kids, and I'd like to help you."

When Henry opened the room door he found that

Shadow had not moved. He didn't bark or whine.

"What a good dog you are, Shadow!" exclaimed Benny. "Here is your supper. I really wish you were my dog. We'll keep your breakfast for you in the bag."

The dog was hungry and ate every crumb. He licked the paper plate several times. Then he lay down again.

"I don't think we will have any trouble with him," Henry said. "He acts tired out and I think he'll sleep. As for me, I'm tired out, too."

It was only eight o'clock. But the Aldens went to bed and went to sleep. Everything was quiet.

Just at midnight Shadow gave a short, sharp bark.

Jessie woke right away. "Oh, dear!" she said. "That's Shadow! Now we'll all have to go! And in the middle of the night, too."

Henry jumped out of bed and ran to the hallway where Shadow was. "Quiet, Shadow!" he said.

Benny sat up and rubbed his eyes. "What time is it?" he asked.

Shadow did not bark again, but he made a growling sound.

"Shh!" Henry said. "It's midnight. Shadow, what is wrong with you?"

By now Benny was awake. "Maybe someone is outside and Shadow hears him," he said.

Shadow gave a short whine now.

Jessie and Violet were standing in their doorway, looking at Shadow and the boys.

Violet said, "Shadow didn't bark for nothing, that's sure. What's the matter, Shadow? Show us."

Shadow seemed to understand. He ran to the outside door and sniffed.

Henry very carefully opened the door just a crack.

"Smoke!" Benny exclaimed. "I smell smoke!"

"Fire somewhere!" Henry said. "Come on, Benny. You girls and Shadow stay right here."

Jessie put her arms around the little dog's neck and held him.

The girls heard Henry and Benny running toward the manager's office.

"I see smoke coming from that lovely dining room!" Violet said. "There's a fire there."

"We'd better stay right here," said Jessie. "This part of the motel isn't in any danger."

Indeed all the smoke was coming from the new dining room. The manager, in a raincoat, ran out in his bare feet. He had a fire extinguisher and turned it on the fire. Other men hurried to help. They turned a fire hose on the fire, and it soon began to die out.

"Not bad," said one man. "We got it before the fire really got going. You're a lucky man, Mister."

"Yes, I am," said the manager. "That part of my motel is new. I'd hate to lose it."

"Who found the fire?" asked a woman.

"Those kids in the end rooms," said the manager. But he didn't say a word about the dog. He had heard Shadow bark. But it seemed no one, except the Aldens, had heard anything.

The manager ran quickly over to the Aldens. He spoke in a low voice. "Your dog saved my motel, kids," he said. "I want you to know that. But I don't

want the people to know there is a dog here. Everybody would want to bring dogs."

"We won't say a word," replied Benny. "And Shadow doesn't care for any glory."

Jessie said, "Besides, we want to be on our way early in the morning."

"Stop for breakfast," said the manager. "Just tell me what you want and what time. I'll get it for you myself. I may not go to bed again. Now that the fire is out, I have to clean up. What would you like for breakfast?"

Benny said, "I'd like a real breakfast. Bacon and eggs and toast and milk and orange juice."

The manager laughed. "How about some sausage?"

"No thanks, I like bacon better."

Henry said, "Maybe we should leave about six o'clock. We have a long day's ride ahead of us."

The manager said, "That would be fine. Then nobody would see the dog, and I wouldn't have to explain. I hope you'll come back again. You did a great thing for me, smelling that smoke in time."

The Aldens went back to sleep and so did Shadow. But the manager could not sleep. He wanted to be sure the fire did not break out again. He was in the dining room with the table set for the children when they came in very quietly.

They had wheeled their bikes over to the dining room, and Henry had Shadow under one arm.

Henry tried to pay the manager for the rooms and meals.

"No," the man said. "I will let you pay for one room but no meals. If you hadn't been here, I wouldn't have any dining room this morning."

"That was Shadow," Benny said.

"Yes, I know. I owe a lot to that dog. But come again sometime without him. You can always spend the night here free."

Benny finished the last of his breakfast and said, "I'm ready. Let's go!"

"We're all ready," Jessie said. "Off we go!"

Shadow wagged his tail. The Aldens had their knapsacks on. They waved to the manager and set off on their bikes. The morning was cool and it was pleasant to ride when there was no traffic.

Sometimes Shadow ran along beside the bikes. Sometimes Henry gave him a ride. He really seemed part of the family.

After miles of riding, Henry said, "Now we are not far from Aunt Jane's."

"Good," said Benny. "Aunt Jane will get us some lunch. Or Maggie. I guess it will be Maggie."

CHAPTER 8

Catch as Catch Can

Benny said suddenly, "Now I know where we are! There's the old lighthouse where we stayed that summer. Remember?"

"That was fun, living in that lighthouse," said Violet.

Henry said, "It shows we are not many miles from Aunt Jane's."

They all looked toward the old lighthouse, but they did not stop.

As they came near Aunt Jane's big farmhouse, they heard a dog barking. Shadow barked in answer.

"That must be Aunt Jane's dog Lady," Violet said. "When Lady was a puppy, we gave her to Aunt Jane. I hope Lady and Shadow won't fight."

Aunt Jane and Uncle Andy waved from the front porch.

"How good to see you!" Aunt Jane said. "We have been looking for you. But Lady saw you first."

Uncle Andy said, "You didn't tell us you were bringing a dog."

Henry held Shadow. "We didn't have a dog then," he said. "We don't want the two dogs to fight." He put Shadow on the grass. The two dogs wagged their tails. They seemed friendly, although they kept on barking.

Then the four Aldens told how they happened to have the dog.

Uncle Andy said, "Here, Shadow, let me see you." He looked carefully at the little dog. "That's a Skye terrier," he said. "Those dogs come from Scotland.

From the island of Skye. That kind of a dog is more than three hundred years old."

"You know everything, Uncle Andy," Benny said.

"Well, boy, I've traveled a lot. You go get that red dictionary in my den. You'll find a good picture of your dog."

Benny soon brought out the red book. "That's Shadow all right," he said. "When we get home we will advertise in the paper, Found: Skye Terrier."

"I wonder how he got lost," said Aunt Jane.

"That's our mystery, Aunt Jane," Jessie said. "You know Benny always has to have a mystery."

"Do you think he was stolen?" Uncle Andy asked. "You said he didn't have a collar."

Henry answered, "We don't know. But that man and woman who stopped in their car thought *we* had stolen him!"

"That's exactly what they thought!" Benny said.

"Let us know what happens to Shadow," said Aunt Jane. "I'm sure you don't know it, but Uncle Andy wants to fly to Spain. He wants me to go with him."

"Right!" Uncle Andy said. "Your Aunt Jane always goes where I go. I'm going to the airport this afternoon to pick up the tickets."

Benny said, "That is just like you, Uncle Andy. Always going somewhere."

"Lunch, kids!" Uncle Andy said next. "I've been waiting for you, and lunch was ready a long time ago."

"Well, I'm ready," said Benny. "You can believe that, Aunt Jane."

"Yes, sir!" Aunt Jane said—she remembered Benny's appetite very well. "It is hard to fill you up."

The Aldens were delighted to see Maggie, who had worked so many years for Aunt Jane. She had made an enormous egg salad for lunch. She had platters of ham, glasses of milk, and hot rolls.

After lunch, Jessie and Violet sat down to talk with Aunt Jane. Henry and Benny rode along with Uncle Andy to the airport. They took Shadow with them. Just as they parked the car, Uncle Andy said, "Look at that!"

A big dog was running across the parking lot for the airport. A man was trying to catch him.

The dog was a boxer. The Aldens could see that the dog didn't want to be caught. The man was having no luck at all.

"Hi!" Benny called. "Come back here and I'll catch your dog for you."

"Oh, Ben, don't say that," said Henry. "You can't catch a strange dog."

"Yes, I think I know a way," said Benny.

The man called, "I can't run after that dog any more. I have to meet a plane and I'm wasting time."

Benny called, "Don't worry. I think I can catch him." He got out of Uncle Andy's car and let Shadow out, too. Shadow began to trot after the big dog.

"Stay!" said Benny. Shadow sat down.

"My," said the stranger. "I wish my dog would mind like that."

"He would," Benny answered, "if he took lessons. Now just wait. Stand behind that little truck where your dog can't see you. Have his leash ready."

The boxer noticed that nobody was chasing him. He looked back and saw Shadow sitting in the parking lot.

The boxer wagged his short tail and trotted back to see the strange dog.

Benny asked the man, "Are you ready? Catch your dog while he is making friends with my dog."

The boxer walked up to Shadow. He wagged his tail. Shadow never moved. He just wagged his tail, too. That was hard because he was sitting on it.

"I'm coming out slowly," the man whispered.

"Right," Benny agreed. Now everyone was watching to see if the man could catch his boxer.

The big dog was so busy making friends with Shadow that he didn't notice when his master snapped the leash on his collar.

"There!" Benny said. "There's your dog."

Uncle Andy said, "That's pretty smart, Benny. I didn't believe you could do that."

"Thanks, boy," said the man. "Now I can meet the plane all right." He put the dog in his car.

A woman had been watching all this time. She said to Henry, "Your dog is a Skye terrier, isn't he?"

"Yes, we think so," replied Henry.

Benny broke in, "He isn't our dog. He just follows us."

The lady looked at Benny. "I just came from Boston," she said. "My sister lives there and she told me a friend of hers had lost a Skye terrier."

Benny shook his head. "This dog could never have come from Boston. We are going to find his owner as soon as we can."

"Good luck," the woman said. "He's a beautiful dog."

That evening Aunt Jane said, "I'm sorry you aren't staying with us longer. But I know you want to get home to solve the mystery of Shadow's owner."

Jessie said, "We were going to stay just one night anyway. We'll come back for a longer visit in the fall."

The next morning the Aldens packed up again. Maggie gave them another set of emergency rations. She said, "Come again soon. I like to have young people around and two barking dogs, too."

The Aldens got on their bikes and rode off as Aunt Jane and Uncle Andy waved good-bye. Lady barked and wagged her tail. Shadow barked, too.

Benny said, "I like to hear you bark, brother. It's much better than whining."

Shadow ran ahead of the bikes. Jessie said, "I believe that dog knows he's going home. He seems glad to go back."

"Maybe that's why Shadow has whined so much," Henry said. "He knew we were going the wrong way. Don't let him run too long, Benny. His paws will get sore."

Benny said, "Pretty soon I'll give him a ride." And in about a half hour, he picked Shadow up and set him in the basket in front of the handlebars.

As they rode along, the four riders began to sing. It was a slow song and they really needed a guitar. When Shadow heard it, he began to howl.

Benny was singing the guitar part, "Plunk, plunk, plunk!" He laughed. "That's what makes you howl, Shadow. I didn't know you could howl." Then he went right along singing.

The minute the song was over, Shadow stopped howling. He just rode along in his basket, looking happy. That made Benny laugh again.

"You win, Shadow," Henry called. "We'll stop singing and you stop howling."

After a few hours of pedaling, Benny said, "Look, we are coming to a crossroad. It looks like heavy traffic ahead!"

CHAPTER 9

Lucky Day

We aren't used to traffic," said Jessie, laughing. "We haven't met many cars, Ben."

Benny said excitedly, "But this one is stopping! Oho! It's trying to stop *us!*"

The car drove up so near the Aldens that they had to get off their bikes.

Jessie whispered, "It's that same man and woman who wanted to buy Shadow—or just take him."

This time both the man and woman got out of their car. The man said, "I've been thinking about you kids. Are you sure you didn't steal this dog?"

"Steal him!" exclaimed Benny. "Of course we didn't steal him! We wouldn't steal anything, not even a penny."

"But you still have a dog that doesn't belong to you. You say that yourselves. We saw you before, remember?"

"Look here," Henry said, "we are on our way home now. We have been trying all the time to find out who owns the dog."

"Well, that's what you say," said the man. "You don't want the police to find you with a missing dog, do you? I know what that dog is worth as a show dog. You'd better sell him to me."

The woman bent over to pat Shadow, but the little dog growled.

Just then another car came along. The driver slowed down and put his head out the window.

"Any trouble over there?" he asked kindly.

"Well, a little," said Henry.

"I say a lot!" exclaimed Benny. "This dog has followed us for four days on our bicycle trip. Now this man says we stole the dog, but we didn't. We are going home now to find the owner."

The stranger looked at the man and woman closely. Then he looked at the Aldens. He said, "Can't you folks see that these young people are telling the truth? I never saw them before, but I would trust them. They look honest to me."

"Well, you can't tell by looks," argued the man. "They have had a strange dog with them for four days, and they don't know where he came from. Maybe they did steal him. Nobody can tell for sure."

"Well," said the man in the car, "I think you had better be on your way. Never mind about the dog. He isn't your dog, either, is he?"

Now the couple saw that the young people had some real help. They turned and got into their car and drove away.

"Look!" said Benny. "Look at their license plates."

Jessie said, "What do you know! Those people are two thousand miles away from their home. That license plate is from the West Coast, and here they are in New England."

Henry nodded. "Maybe *they* are the ones who try to pick up dogs. People do steal dogs and sell them."

"Did you get their license number?" asked the stranger, starting his motor.

"I did," said Violet.

"I did," said Benny. "I can remember it."

"I wrote it down myself," the stranger said. "I don't think they will bother you again. But if they should, here is my card with my name and address." He handed a card to Henry.

The Aldens read the card. It said Hartman's Detective Agency.

Benny asked, "Are you a plainclothes detective, Mr. Hartman?"

"Well, something like that," replied the man with a smile.

Violet said, "Oh, I am so glad you came along. I

don't like trouble, and those people seem to be trying to make trouble for us."

Jessie said, "We certainly thank you for taking our part."

"You're very welcome. Glad I could help," said Mr. Hartman, driving away.

The Aldens stood still for a minute and watched the car drive out of sight.

"Well, I'm all tired out!" said Benny crossly. "All that fuss over a nice little dog. Makes me mad!"

Jessie looked closely at Benny. He did not say things like this very often. "I'll tell you what we'll do," she said. "Let's eat lunch early. That will be something different to do. Just look for a place to eat."

They all agreed that this was a good idea, and they pedaled off down the road. Shadow was glad, too. He ran ahead, barking. Violet came last.

A mile later, the others heard Violet call, "Wait!"

They stopped and Jessie called back, "What is it, Violet?"

"I've got a flat tire," said Violet. "I must have run over something very sharp."

Henry looked at the tire. "I should say you did. It's a sharp stone shaped just like an arrow. The tire is cut through. It will have to be fixed before you can ride on it."

"A new tire might be better," Jessie said.

Benny said, "Well, I guess this isn't our day. We'll have to find a place that fixes bikes. It would be neat if we could find a repair shop that serves meals. Or a restaurant that mends bikes."

The others had to laugh as they all walked along pushing their bicycles.

Jessie was glad that Benny could make jokes again, but she wondered how far they would have to walk to find a repair shop.

They all looked down every side road and at every sign along the way. After a mile or so, they saw a big building in the distance. Soon they could read the sign, "Stop at Big Jeko's Place."

"Look," said Jessie. "Is that a gas station?"

"I don't know," replied Henry. "It looks like a junk shop to me."

But in a minute a big giant of a man looked out of the open door. "Trouble?" he called. "Come in and I see."

Violet gave him her bicycle and they all watched him anxiously. Then Big Jeko nodded and smiled, "I fix quick. You going far?"

"Yes," replied Henry. "We're going to Greenfield."

"I know Greenfield," said the man. "Too far away. Maybe I fix tire and maybe it come off. I guess a new tire for this bike."

"I think so, too," agreed Henry. "Have you a tire the right size?"

"All sizes." Big Jeko took down a tire hanging on the wall and began to take off the old one.

Violet said, "It's my bike. I'm glad you can fix it."

Big Jeko went on working. He said, "I come from Bulgaria. Speak poor English. But you are good kids. Not like some. A good dog, too."

Shadow was indeed a good dog. He sat still and waited without a whine. He sniffed the air.

Violet said, "Mr. Jeko, we were looking for a restaurant when I had my flat tire. Do you know a good place to eat?"

The big man laughed. "Yes, I know. Right here. Big Jeko's Place."

"You mean you serve meals here?" exclaimed

Benny. He looked around curiously. He didn't see any place where they could eat.

"No. Just today I serve lunch for you. Look in there." He pointed to the back room.

Benny and Jessie looked in. Something smelled delicious. There was an old-fashioned stove with a black kettle on top. A woman turned around and smiled at the Aldens. "You like pilaf?" she said. "You stay for pilaf."

The Aldens looked at each other. Jessie said, "I don't know why not. Let's stay, Henry."

Big Jeko's wife said, "Good. Sit down, please." She took four bowls off a shelf.

Then she put the pilaf into each bowl. "You eat," she said to the Aldens. "Here, dog." She put a big lamb bone on the floor for Shadow. There was a lot of meat on it.

The lunch was made of rice and lamb and onions and tomatoes and all sorts of delicious things, just what the Alden children liked. They ate the pilaf with pieces of hard bread.

When they had finished eating, they all thanked the woman and went out into the shop. The bike was fixed, and Henry paid Big Jeko for the tire and the lunch.

Then Big Jeko surprised them. He said, "You like dog show? Dog show here in Ashby? I have tickets."

"You have tickets to sell?" asked Jessie. "We have heard of the dog show in Ashby."

"I have lots of tickets," Big Jeko replied. "I make all the cages for dogs. I make wire cages." He pointed to some square cages in the corner. "Then they give me lots of tickets."

Benny said, "Oh, we could use four tickets. This dog with us is a show dog. He ought to be in the show, really."

"Yes, I know," said Big Jeko. "Good show dog." He handed four tickets to Henry.

The Aldens shook hands with Big Jeko and got on their bikes. "We won't forget you, Mr. Jeko," said Violet. "You were so kind to us."

They all waved good-bye and rode away.

"I take it all back about our day," said Benny. "We got our lunch, we got the bike fixed, and now we have four tickets to the dog show. It's our lucky day, after all."

CHAPTER 10

One Puzzle Left

Now the Aldens wanted nothing but to
_____ They agreed not to stop any-
_____ sleep.
_____ say hello to Mrs. Randall,
_____ ough Second Landing."
_____ hat. We told her we might."

They rode along steadily for the rest of the trip. On the last morning it was almost lunchtime when Shadow started to run away.

"Come back!" shouted Benny. But Shadow had no idea of coming back.

Benny yelled, "I thought you were an obedient dog. Don't you understand? Come back!"

Shadow was not listening. He was running for dear life.

Henry watched him for a minute. Then he quietly, "We must follow him. We can't lo now."

The four children pedaled up with the running dog.

"He'll hurt his paws, He you carry him?"

"No, I don't think I can d "He thinks he's going hon feet go!"

"Wait for us!" Benny stop for an instant.

"He's going right for Second Landing," Jessie said. "Mr. Martin's store is ahead. You don't suppose he belongs to Mr. Martin, do you?"

"No, I don't," said Henry. "Mr. Martin didn't act as if he had lost a beautiful show dog."

"It couldn't be the Randalls," Benny put in. "They ___ as if they had lost a dog either. I didn't see ___ the floor. And there wasn't any dog-___ ard."

said ___ se him

___ adow acts as if Second Landing is home,"

___ ed along.

___ away u ___ Mr. "Look at

___ Mar Hi, Mr.

___ ry," s ___ Th

___ tle wa ran a lit-

___ atch ___ "Th

___ e, ___ "How claimed.

___ Benn

___ pened," hat hap-

___ ay."

Then Mr. Martin saw the dog. The Aldens were astonished to see him stand up and call, "Here, Smoky! Come here, Smoky!"

"Smoky!" Jessie exclaimed. "Do you know this dog, Mr. Martin?"

"I should say so! That's the Randalls' dog."

"The *Randalls*?"

"Well, he doesn't belong to the family," Mr. Martin said. "He belongs to Carl. His Uncle Eric gave the dog to him for his birthday. See, he wants you to come!"

Shadow ran a little way and looked back. The Aldens got on their bikes and followed him. Now at last Shadow did not whine.

Mr. Martin called after them, "You'll find a happy family when they see that dog."

As the Aldens knew, it was not far to the Randalls' house. The little dog barked, and Benny ran up on the porch to knock at the door.

Mrs. Randall came to the door and took one look. "Oh, Smoky, Smoky!" she cried. She opened the door

and the little dog jumped into her arms. He wiggled, squealing and whining and licking her hands.

The Aldens stood and watched. In a minute Mrs. Randall looked up with tears in her eyes. "Oh, thank you for bringing him back," she said. "But how did you know whose dog he was?"

"We didn't," Jessie said. "It's a long story. We have been trying to find out who owns Shadow ever since he came to us."

"Do come in and sit down. You see my brother Eric gave this dog to Carl for his birthday. Smoky was all trained and ready to be entered in the dog show at Ashby. We had him only a week, but we grew to love him."

"So did we," said Violet.

They all sat down and watched the dog. He was running all over the house, smelling everything and coming back to Mrs. Randall.

"Your picture was in the paper this morning," said Mrs. Randall. "I was sure it was Smoky standing with you. I was trying to think how to find you."

"I know who took that picture," said Benny. "A man and a woman followed us and tried to get Smoky away from us. They want people to think we stole the dog. What did it say under the picture?"

"Not very much," said Mrs. Randall. "Just 'Bicycle dog lost.' Several people called me to tell me they were sure it was Carl's dog."

"There! You see," said Benny, "that is why that couple took our picture. Just to make people think we stole the dog. And we think *they* are the ones who pick up dogs."

Mrs. Randall said, "I still don't know where you found Smoky."

The Aldens told her about the old empty house and the rain and the little whining dog.

"He followed us to Aunt Jane's and all the way back," said Jessie. "But we still don't understand how you lost him!"

"Well," Mrs. Randall began. "You remember that Carl had gone to camp just the day before you came? After Carl had left on the bus, I had some special shopping to do that day. I put Smoky in the station wagon and drove to a shopping center. It was a big place about twenty-five miles in the other direction. I couldn't take Smoky into the stores, so I left him in the car. I rolled down one of the windows to give him some air."

The Aldens nodded.

"Yes, that was a mistake," Mrs. Randall agreed. "Smoky wiggled out of that window somehow, although I don't see how he could. Anyway, when I came out, he was gone!"

"Did anyone see him?" asked Violet.

"Nobody that I could ask," said Mrs. Randall. "There were hundreds of cars. I called and called, but at last I had to drive home."

"Poor Carl," said Violet. "Did you have to tell him Smoky was missing?"

"No, I just hoped and hoped Smoky would come home. But he had been here such a short time, I didn't think he would know how to get home. And I was afraid someone would find him and keep him."

Jessie said, "And you had all this to worry about that day we came to help. We noticed you were upset about something. Why didn't you tell us?"

"I just couldn't," Mrs. Randall said. "I didn't want to spoil everything, and we were having such a good time. And I knew I might break down and tell the company."

"That was Mr. Evans," Benny said. "He would always understand. You can tell Carl now."

"Yes, he gets home tomorrow. What a lot of news I shall have to tell him! Smoky lost, and Smoky found. And we are moving to Boston right away."

"Good," said Jessie. Her eyes twinkled. "I'm glad Mr. Evans found out that you were a friendly person."

"I'm going to telephone Eric. He will be so pleased. Now we can show Smoky in the Ashby dog show. I do hope you can go to that show. It will be exciting."

"Yes," said Benny. "We have four tickets."

"You are lucky. They are hard to get. And Smoky is lucky that he found you instead of somebody else."

"Well," said Benny. "Now I know what a lucky dog is!"

The Aldens got up to go home. Mrs. Randall said, "I'll remind you of the dog show a little later. I'll call you up."

As the Aldens rode home, Henry said, "There's still a mystery to solve. What happened to Smoky between the time he was left in the Randall car in the parking lot and came to the old house in the rain?"

"Yes, I was thinking about that, too," said Benny.

CHAPTER 11

Show Dog

The Aldens reached home safely. They found that their grandfather knew all about the dog. He had seen their picture in the paper. But Violet had to tell him all about the rainy night in the empty house. Jessie told him about the roadside stand and Roy Smith. Benny told him about Big Jeko.

At last Mr. Alden said, "Were you satisfied with all those adventures, Ben?"

"Well, almost," Benny replied. "There's just one thing about this mystery that we don't know. How did Smoky get from the parking lot to the empty house where we spent the night?"

"I can't help you there," Mr. Alden said. "But I have no doubt you four will solve that, too."

Later on, Jessie had a telephone call from Mrs. Randall.

She said, "The Ashby dog show begins tomorrow. We are going to show Smoky. Our little dog has a new name, but I promised not to tell you. Can you come?"

Jessie laughed. She said, "Yes, I don't even need to ask the others. We'll be delighted to drive over to the show."

"Come to our house first," said Mrs. Randall. "Then you can meet Carl. And we will all go in two cars."

"We'll be there," Jessie said.

"Fine," said Mrs. Randall. "I want you to see Eric show off the dog. It's quite a sight."

The next day, as Henry drove along, Benny said, "I give up about that new name for Smoky. I'm sure they wouldn't call him Shadow just because we did."

"We'll have to wait and see," Violet said.

When the Aldens reached the Randalls' yard, Carl ran out. He was a freckled boy in a Camp Mohawk shirt.

"You must be the Alden kids!" he called. "I'm Carl."

They all went into the house, and Carl's Uncle Eric shook hands with the Aldens.

"Tell me," said Uncle Eric, "how did the dog get to you after he left the parking lot?"

"We'd like to know that," answered Jessie. "I wonder if we'll ever know."

"Oh, we'll know sometime!" said Benny.

Carl said, "Wait until you see how fine Smoky looks. He's been washed and brushed. His paws and toes are cleaned and shined."

"I can't wait to see him!" Violet said.

"What about his new name?" Benny asked.

"You have to wait for that," Carl said with a wink. "It's time to go now."

Henry followed the Randall car to Ashby. He had a little trouble parking, so the Randalls went in first with Smoky.

The Ashby dog show was held in a big hall. When the Aldens went in, they saw the steward standing right by the door.

He said to the young people, "Come in. Your friends are right over there." He pointed to a large sign that said "Class—Skye Terrier." Under the sign were two cages.

"That steward seemed to know us," said Benny. "That's funny."

"Look!" Violet said. "Read what it says on Smoky's cage. There's Smoky's new name!"

A big sign was printed with the words, "Smoky, the Bicycle Dog."

People were standing around Smoky's cage.

Someone said, "That's the dog that was stolen."

Another said, "He wasn't stolen."

"Who stole the Bicycle Dog?"

"What are you talking about?"

"Didn't you read about it in the paper? Four children on bicycles found him."

Mrs. Randall smiled at the Aldens. She said, "I guess you don't know that everyone has seen the picture of you riding your bikes, with Smoky beside you. Tomorrow we will put another piece in the paper telling that you *found* the dog. Nobody stole him."

Smoky was delighted to see the Aldens. He tried to get out of his cage, but he could not. He licked their hands through the wires.

"That cage makes me think of Big Jeko," said Violet.

"It won't be long now," said Uncle Eric. "I am going to handle Smoky. But don't forget, he is Carl's dog. Next year he can handle him."

"What do you mean, handle?" asked Benny. "I would think anyone could handle Smoky."

"You'll see," Uncle Eric replied. "It means to

show him off. The dog has to know what he is expected to do, too."

The Aldens noticed there was one other dog in the same class with Smoky. It was a Skye terrier named Cinderella, for cinder, the color of ashes. It was a soft bluish-gray dog.

Then the show began. The four Aldens found places with the crowd behind the rope.

Everyone was excited. Everyone wanted his dog to get a first prize. Of course, everyone thought that Smoky, the Bicycle Dog, would win a first prize.

Dogs of all kinds were there. There were enormous dogs with soft white fur, and tiny dogs no bigger than a man's hand. All of them were trained.

The first dog was a Great Dane. His master held his leash while the band played. The dog walked slowly. Then he stood still with his head up and his tail down.

Then came Cinderella. "My," said Jessie, "hear the people clap!"

And then came Smoky. Uncle Eric knew exactly

what to do, and so did Smoky. Henry said, "Now hear them clap! Even louder than for Cinderella."

The judges for the dog show watched every dog closely. They noticed how the dogs looked and how they acted.

Later on, the judges went around putting ribbons on the cages. The crowd followed them to see which dogs were winners. Then what a surprise! Nobody could believe it. Smoky, the Bicycle Dog, had the second prize, a red ribbon, and the blue ribbon went to Cinderella!

Carl said, "Well, never mind. I like red better than blue anyway."

"I don't," said Uncle Eric. "But I'm not surprised."

"Aren't *you* surprised?" Jessie asked Mrs. Randall.

"No. I'll explain. Smoky's trip didn't do him any good. He wasn't dried when he got wet in the rain. He wasn't washed. A dog must be in perfect condition to win the blue ribbon in this show."

"But wait till next year!" said Uncle Eric.

Suddenly Ben said, "Look—twins! Exactly alike."

"One in pink and one in blue," said Violet in a low voice.

Jessie said, "They are coming this way. I think they are looking for Smoky."

A smiling woman and the two little girls came through the crowd.

"We want to see our dog," said the twin in pink. "My name is Laurie."

"Your dog?" asked Benny. "You mean the Bicycle Dog?"

"Well, he isn't really ours. But we saw him twice, and we wanted him very much. My name is Joy."

The lady said, "We are the Fullers. My girls just love that dog. They saw him in a parking lot in Essex."

"Oh, yes," said Laurie. "He was running around the parking lot."

"Where were you?" asked Uncle Eric.

"We were in the back of the station wagon," replied Joy. "We can see everything. We called him and called him, but he ran off. Then we saw the same dog at a vegetable stand way out in the country."

"Well," said Benny, "that settles that. Nobody stole him."

"But they tried to, Ben," Henry said. "Don't forget that."

"I'll never forget that," said Benny.

Then Uncle Eric said, "Did you girls see what happened to Smoky that day in the parking lot?"

"Oh, yes," said Laurie.

"Oh, no," said Joy. "All we know is that he ran out of the parking lot and right across the road."

"And he wasn't even run over," Laurie added.

"No," agreed Uncle Eric without a smile. "I should say he got across the road safely. You don't know which way he went after that?"

"Oh, yes, we know which *way* he went. Do you know that shortcut in Essex to the old back road? Well, that's where he was going. Right to that old country road."

"We hoped he would find his way home, because the next night it rained. Did you find him?"

"He found us," said Benny. "He climbed in our window to get out of the rain. On that old country road."

Henry asked, "And you saw him again at a roadside stand?"

"That's right," said Joy. "My father says Smoky will get first prize in any dog show next year. We want to say hello to him."

Smoky seemed to know the little twins. He tried to get out of the cage, and he licked their hands and whined.

A policeman had been walking around the show all day. Now he came walking up to the Aldens. He said to Henry, "You kids want to help me? I hear that you had a bit of trouble with a man and a woman who tried to get your dog."

"That's right," Henry answered.

"Would you know them again, if you saw them?" asked the officer.

"We would!" said Benny.

The officer looked at the four Aldens and smiled.

He said, "Well, we have a couple at the police station. Tomorrow will you come with me and tell me if they are the same ones you saw?"

"We certainly will," answered Henry.

"That's all I want," the officer said with a wink. "You all agree?"

"Yes, sir," Jessie said. "They tried twice to get the dog."

"Good," the policeman said. "We found them with two stolen poodles and a Scottie that didn't belong to them. That man and woman will go back where they came from, but they will pay a great big fine!"

"They deserve it!" Benny said. "I hope they won't do it again."

"They won't," promised the man. He laughed. "They have policemen on the West Coast, too, you know." He turned and went away.

Jessie said, "Well, Mrs. Fuller, you heard that. I guess things will be all right now."

The dog show was over. Everyone was packing

up to go. The Randalls went home with Smoky and the Aldens went straight home to Greenfield.

Grandfather met them on the front porch. "How was the show?" he asked.

The four young people sat down on the porch and told Mr. Alden the whole story.

Violet told about Smoky's new name and how the twins had helped solve the last puzzle.

Benny said, "But I'm awfully disappointed that Smoky didn't get the first prize. People liked him the best."

"I'm sorry myself," said Grandfather. "But there was a reason. And don't forget, Ben, somebody always has to come in second."

And this was something Benny Alden never forgot.

Then Watch came out to see his children. Benny opened the screen door and let him out. He lay down on the porch.

Benny said, "Hello, Watch." He knelt down and scratched the dog's rough head. Watch lifted his nose.

Benny said, "I like you best, Watch. You don't whine or yelp or howl or bark."

Then they all had to laugh, because what did Watch do? He barked!

GERTRUDE CHANDLER WARNER discovered when she was teaching that many readers who like an exciting story could find no books that were both easy and fun to read. She decided to try to meet this need, and her first book, *The Boxcar Children*, quickly proved she had succeeded.

Miss Warner drew on her own experiences to write the mystery. As a child she spent hours watching trains go by on the tracks opposite her family home. She often dreamed about what it would be like to set up housekeeping in a caboose or freight car—the situation the Alden children find themselves in.

When Miss Warner received requests for more adventures involving Henry, Jessie, Violet, and Benny Alden, she began additional stories. In each, she chose a special setting and introduced unusual or eccentric characters who liked the unpredictable.

While the mystery element is central to each of Miss Warner's books, she never thought of them as strictly juvenile mysteries. She liked to stress the Aldens' independence and resourcefulness and their solid New England devotion to using up and making do. The Aldens go about most of their adventures with as little adult supervision as possible—something else that delights young readers.

Miss Warner lived in Putnam, Connecticut, until her death in 1979. During her lifetime, she received hundreds of letters from girls and boys telling her how much they liked her books. And so she continued the Aldens' adventures, writing a total of nineteen books in the Boxcar Children series.